Lake, WI 54810

THE LIBRARY OF BATS™

VAMPIRE BATS

EMILY RAABE

The Rosen Publishing Group's
PowerKids Press™
New York

For Bob and Bob, with love

Published in 2003 by The Rosen Publishing Group, Inc.
29 East 21st Street, New York, NY 10010

First Edition

Editor: Natashya Wilson
Book Design: Emily Muschinske

Photo Credits: Cover, pp. 1, 7 (top right, bottom left and right), 11 (all photos), 12, 14 (all photos), 15, 18 (top left), 19, 20 © Roger Rageot/David Liebman; p. 4 © The Everett Collection; pp. 5, 13, 21 © Robert and Linda Mitchell; p. 7 (top left) © Roger W. Barbour/National Museum of Natural History/Smithsonian Institution; pp. 7 (center), 17 © Michael & Patricia Fogden/CORBIS; p. 8 (top) © ANT Photo Library; p. 8 (bottom) © Merlin D. Tuttle, Bat Conservation International; p. 9 © Gary Braasch/CORBIS; p. 19 (inset) Eric DePalo; back cover (top right) © Digital Stock; back cover (left) © CORBIS.

Raabe, Emily.
Vampire bats / Emily Raabe.— 1st ed.
    p. cm. — (The library of bats)
Includes bibliographical references (p.   ).
Summary: An introduction to the vampire bat, best known for its diet which consists of the blood of other animals.
ISBN 0-8239-6322-5 (library binding)
1. Vampire bats—Juvenile literature. [1. Vampire bats. 2. Bats.] I. Title. II. Series.
QL737.C52 R235 2003
599.4'5—dc21

                                    2001005335

Manufactured in the United States of America

CONTENTS

VAMPIRE!

Vampire bats! The name might make you think of giant bats flying across a full moon with blood on their fangs. Vampire bats are not big bats. They don't fly across full moons, because darkness hides them better. However, they are some of the most amazing kinds of bats. Like all bats, vampire bats are **mammals**. Humans, tigers, and rabbits are examples of other mammals. Unlike any other mammal, vampire bats eat only blood. To get this blood, they have to be quick and quiet. Vampire bats have good eyesight. They fly, crawl, and jump. They have strong senses of smell and hearing. A flying vampire bat can hear a sleeping animal breathing in a field!

The word "vampire," or "vampyre," is a very old word that means "blood drunkenness." This vampire bat is drinking a meal of blood from a bowl.

BAT FACT

The word "vampire" was used in stories of people who rose from the dead to drink the blood of the living long before it became a name for blood-drinking bats. In 1498, the explorer Christopher Columbus said he had seen giant, blood-sucking bats in South America. Since then vampire bats have become the subjects of legends and movies.

Tiny Blood Eaters

If you see a vampire bat, you might be surprised at its size. Vampire bats are only about the size of small mice. When vampire bats appear in movies, the movie people usually use a bat called a flying fox to play the vampire bat. This is because flying foxes are much bigger than vampire bats. Vampire bats are usually gray, but they also can be a dull brown color. Scientists have reported seeing orange vampire bats. There are three **species**, or kinds, of vampire bats. These three species are the common vampire bat, the white-winged vampire bat, and the hairy-legged vampire bat. White-winged and hairy-legged vampire bats are rare. When people talk about vampire bats, they are almost always talking about the common vampire bat.

Bat Stats

Vampire bats' wings are from 13 to 14 inches (33–35.5 cm) long from tip to tip. These bats weigh about 1 ½ ounces (42.5 g). Flying foxes' wings can be 5 ½ feet (2 m) long from tip to tip!

The common vampire bat (center) and the hairy-legged vampire bat (bottom left) are closely related to the other bats pictured here.

LONG-NOSED BAT

YELLOW-EARED BAT

COMMON VAMPIRE BAT

HAIRY-LEGGED VAMPIRE BAT

FRUIT BAT

FALSE VAMPIRE BATS

Vampire bats like hot, wet weather. They live in south Texas, **tropical** Mexico, Central America, and South America. Although there are only three kinds of vampire bats, there are many other bats that were once mistakenly called vampire bats by scientists. These bats live in Central America, South America, Asia, and Australia. Some of these other bats are grouped into a **family** called false vampire bats. Most false vampire bats are much larger than true vampire bats. None of them live on blood the way true vampire bats do, but all of them are **carnivores**. Scientists thought that false vampire bats drank blood, because they are so fierce looking.

BAT FACT

There are other bats that do not belong to the official false vampire bat family but that also were mistaken for vampire bats. Linnaeus' false vampire bat *(above)*, has a fearsome-looking face. That may be why it was thought to be a vampire bat. It actually belongs to the American leaf-nosed bat family.

The ghost bat is a false vampire bat that lives in northern Australia. It has a wingspan of about 2 feet (.6 m). Ghost bats eat mice, birds, insects, lizards, and even other bats!

THE ACROBAT

Vampire bats are the **acrobats** of the bat world. Vampire bats can crawl up or down walls as well as fly. They can tiptoe on the backs of sleeping cows or hop out of the way of swishing tails or stamping hooves. They can bounce like rubber balls or can stand up and look around, like tiny monkeys. Many vampire bats can fly after eating their own weight in blood. Vampire bats can move in so many different ways, because they have special thumbs that work like two extra feet. These thumbs are very long, and each thumb has three pads on it. A vampire bat can walk on these pads in the same way that an ape uses its knuckles to walk upright. It also can push off with its pads and leap into the air.

BAT STATS

Vampire bats rarely wake their sleeping victims, but they need to be able to escape quickly, just in case! They can run up to 5 miles per hour (8 km/h).

A vampire bat's skeleton (bottom right) helps it to move easily. The bat's long thumb (top right) can be used like a foot (bottom left) to help the bat run and jump. This vampire bat (top left) is ready to leap into the air.

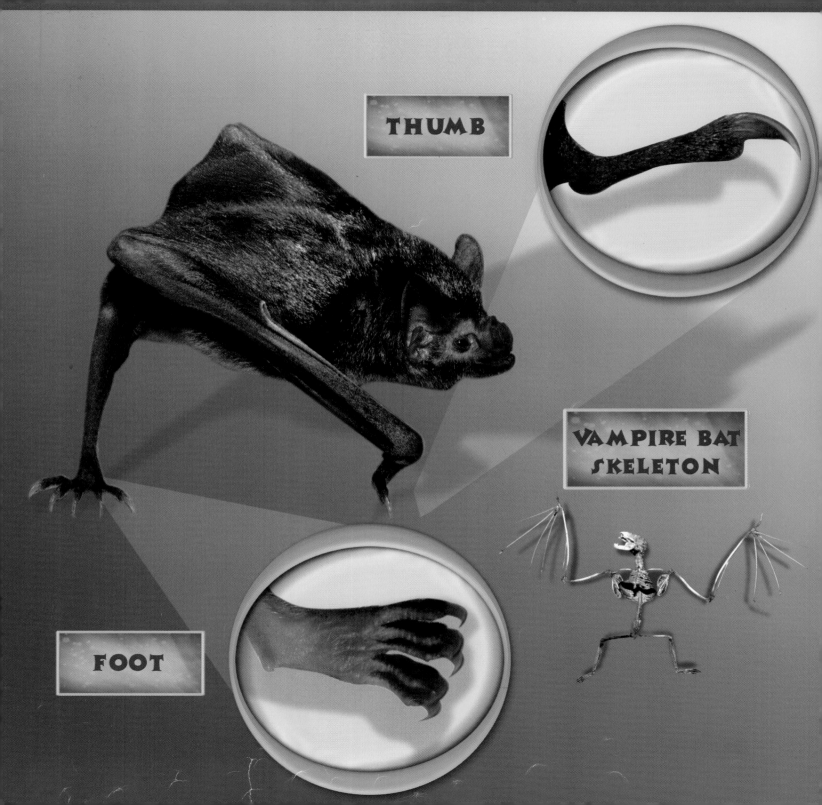

THUMB

VAMPIRE BAT
SKELETON

FOOT

Vampire bats leave their **roosts** in the dark of night to hunt for blood. They use something called **echolocation** to find their way around in darkness. Echolocation is sending out pulses of sound and listening to the echo of the sound when it hits an object. Bats that echolocate can tell how close or how far away an object is by the amount of time it takes for the echo to return to them. Vampire bats also use their hearing and sense of smell to find sleeping animals. A vampire bat will land on or near a sleeping animal. Then the bat creeps around on the animal's body until it finds the right spot from which to bite the animal.

BAT FACT

Although vampire bats usually take blood from livestock, such as cows or horses, they also like human blood. If a vampire bat bites a sleeping human, it usually bites the body parts that stick out, such as the toes, the nose, or the tips of the person's ears!

The vampire bat has heat sensors on its nose. These heat sensors help the bat to find a sleeping animal, and then to find a spot on the animal's body where the blood runs close to the skin.

THE SILENT MEAL

Once a vampire bat has picked its victim for the night, it uses its sharp teeth to clip the hair around the spot where it will bite. Then, using its two pointed front teeth, it makes a small cut, about ⅕ inch (5 mm) deep and ⅕ inch (5 mm) wide, from which to get blood. A vampire bat does not actually suck blood. Instead it puts its long tongue into the cut that it has made. It then uses **channels** that run underneath the tongue to lap up the blood and to sip it the way you might sip soda through a drinking straw. A vampire bat will eat 2 tablespoons (29.5 cc) of blood in a feeding, about 60 percent of its own body weight.

In the vampire bat jaw (top left) and skull (top right), and in the live vampire bat (bottom), the front teeth are sharp and close together. This helps the bats to make neat cuts when they bite. The bats' victims feel nothing.

BAT FACT

This cow has been fed upon by a vampire bat. Vampire bats will often return to the same animal night after night. When one bat picks an animal, many other vampire bats usually feed on the unlucky animal as well. Scientists do not know why vampire bats choose one animal instead of another.

A Diet of Blood

Vampire bats need blood. If a vampire bat goes for two days without blood, it may starve to death. Everything about a vampire bat, from its sharp teeth to its special tongue, has been **adapted** for getting and eating blood. Even the vampire bat's saliva, or spit, is made for a blood meal. While a vampire bat is feeding, it mixes its saliva into the victim's blood. Ingredients in the bat's saliva keep the blood flowing from the tiny wound. Vampire bats have special stomachs with thin, stretchy walls that can expand to hold a lot of blood. The bats begin to **urinate** soon after eating, to get rid of wastes. This helps the bats become light enough to fly back home.

Bat Stats

A vampire bat's saliva allows a wound that would normally stop bleeding in 2 to 5 minutes to bleed for 20 minutes or longer. A vampire bat can eat its entire night's meal from one small cut.

Vampire bats have fewer teeth than do other bats. This is because they do not need to chew their food. Instead they need a space in their mouths through which they can stick their tongues to sip blood.

HOME FOR A VAMPIRE BAT

BAT FACT

Vampire bats share food. This is something that no other bats do. If a vampire bat is not able to get blood one night, it will beg for blood from another vampire bat by grooming it and squeaking. The other bat will throw up blood for the hungry vampire bat. Food sharing helps vampire bats survive.

When a vampire bat has finished its evening meal, it will fly home to its roost. Vampire bats spend up to 80 percent of their time resting in their roosts, which might be in caves, in abandoned mine shafts, or even in hollow trees. A group of vampire bats in a roost usually includes one male and from 8 to 20 female bats and their babies. The bats spend a lot of time **grooming** one another in the roosts. You probably wouldn't want to visit a vampire bat roost. This is because the floor of the roost is also the bathroom. Vampire bats eat blood and then **excrete** it, so the floors of their roosts are covered in pools of rotting blood!

This cave is a vampire bat roost. The map (inset) shows where vampire bats live throughout North America, Central America, and South America.

VAMPIRE
BAT HOMES

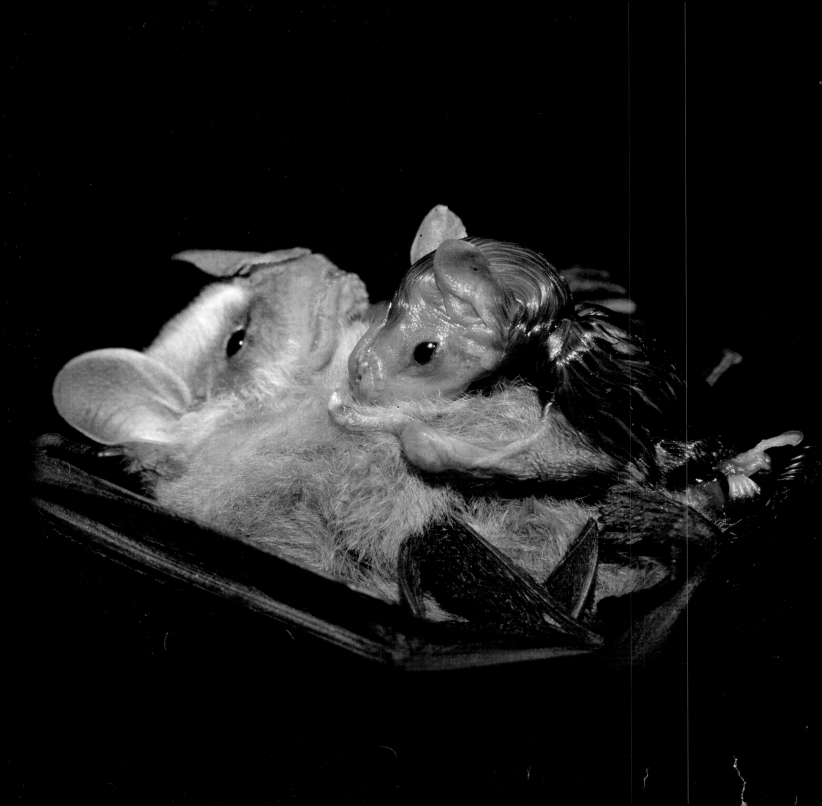

BABY VAMPIRE BATS

Each female vampire bat usually gives birth to only one baby every year. The baby is born with its eyes open. It is bald, and its tiny wings are pink and weak. The baby vampire bat gets a mixture of milk and blood from its mother. The mother vampire bat will carry her baby with her when she hunts. When the baby gets too heavy to carry, it will be left in the roost with the other young vampire bats while the mothers hunt. Baby vampire bats learn to fly by four months of age and begin to go with their mothers on hunting trips. They continue to nurse for up to nine months, however. This is at least six months longer than most baby bats nurse.

BAT FACT

About half of all new vampire bat babies will die during their first year. Vampire babies are not very good at getting blood and often will return home with an empty stomach. However, vampire bats share food, so many more young vampire bats survive than would if they did not share with one another.

As with vampire bat babies, yellow-eared bat babies like this one are bald and pink when they are born. Yellow-eared bats are closely related to vampire bats.

Vampire Bats and People

Vampire bats do not have many enemies. Owls and other bats sometimes hunt them. If a vampire bat gets stuck outside in the daylight, a bat falcon or a brown jay might eat it. People pose the biggest threat to vampire bats. They kill many vampire bats every year to protect farm animals from bites. Most bats are useful to people, because bats eat insects, or help to **pollinate** plants. However, vampire bats bite animals and even people every night. Like any other mammal, vampire bats can carry a disease called rabies, which is spread through bites. In Central America and South America, many farm animals die every year from rabies that they caught from vampire bat bites. Despite the efforts of humans who kill vampire bats, these amazing bats continue to survive. They rule the night air as they hunt for fresh blood.

Bat Stats

Few people get rabies from bats. The total number of rabies cases from all areas where vampire bats live is about 10 people every year. However, if you see a bat on the ground, don't touch it!

GLOSSARY

acrobats (A-kruh-bats) Those who have good control of their bodies and can tumble, leap, flip over, and change positions quickly.

adapted (uh-DAPT-id) To have changed in order to survive better.

carnivores (KAR-nih-vorz) Animals that eat other animals for food.

channels (CHA-nuhlz) Grooves or passageways cut into something to allow a liquid to pass through.

echolocation (eh-koh-loh-KAY-shun) A method of locating objects by producing a sound and judging the time it takes the echo to return and the direction from which it returns. Bats, dolphins, porpoises, killer whales, and some shrews all use echolocation.

excrete (eks-KREET) To get rid of, to pass through the body.

family (FAM-lee) The scientific name for a group of plants or animals that are alike in some ways.

grooming (GROOM-ing) Brushing and cleaning someone's body and making it neat and tidy.

mammals (MA-mulz) Warm-blooded animals that have backbones, often are covered with hair, breathe air, and feed milk to their young.

pollinate (PAH-lih-nayt) To spread pollen from one plant to another so that the plants can reproduce.

roosts (ROOSTS) Places where bats or birds make their homes.

species (SPEE-sheez) A single kind of plant or animal. Humans are one species.

tropical (TRAH-pih-kuhl) Areas that are warm year-round.

urinate (YUR-ih-nayt) To pass liquid wastes from the body.

Index

Web Sites

To learn more about vampire bats, check out these Web sites:

www.angelfire.com/va/vampirebats/
www.jaguarpaw.com/Bats.html
www.thewildones.org/Animals/vampire.html